AMBER TAMBLYN

free Stallion

poems

Simon & Schuster

New York London Toronto Sydney

SIMON & SCHUSTER

1230 Avenue of the Americas, New York, New York 10020

Book design by Einav Aviram

The text for this book is set in Rotis.

Manufactured in the United States of America

10 9 8 7 6 5 4 3 2 1

Library of Congress Cataloging-in-Publication Data

Tamblyn, Amber.

Free stallion : poems / Amber Tamblyn.

p. cm.

ISBN-13: 978-1-4424-3087-7

1. Young adult poetry, American. I. Title.

PS3620.A66F74 2005

811'.6—dc22

2004029152

Dedicated to Jack Hirschman,
deep in the "you know what"

ACKNOWLEDGMENTS

My grandmother Sally, for her immortal beauty. My grandfather Alex, for his hardy Scottish heart and violin. My two other grandparents, Marian and Eddie, who I never knew physically, but still see almost every day. Tin Tin, Rudy, and all my Clann, Murrays and Tamblyns alike. My moo, Bonnie, who sits in Council daily with the young, and whose guitar and voice set the rhythm in my blood (the O.G.A.D.). My father, Russ, simply, for teaching love and perspective. Glenda; Uncle Larry; my sister, China—we are welded for life; Elton; Dylan Pickle; and Vivian Raquel, the queen of tigers.

Billy Williams, Raymond Travis, and San Francisco—keep my heart, you've earned it. My girls: Michaela, Brianne, Mandy, and Juliet. The Girardi family and JOA crew. Leslie Charleson, Stuart Damon, and the Qs. Beyond Baroque for their love and support. The Bernthals, Laurel Schmidt, Madeline Leavitt, Kenzo, Jamy, the Nolan/O'Brien Clann, The Courtyard, Tommy, Sheila, and Chi. Martha Meredith Masters—just for being born with that name (when will you give up your day job for that night one?); David Lust; and The Femme-Bots: Leanne, Joan of Hyler, and Courtney.

George Herms for rust-love, and Pixie, you are one "smart apos!"; Neil; Amber Jean; Pegi; and my Greendale family (Art Green walks among you);

Michael McClure; Wanda Coleman; Lawrence Ferlinghetti; Diane Di Prima; Bruce Conner; Dean Stockwell; David Lynch; Dennis Hopper; and the king of ALL wolves, Wallace Berman. Alexandra Cooper, David Gale, and my family at Simon & Schuster for all the support. Brian Lipson and everyone at Endeavor. Bernie Pock, Ani DiFranco (Pick me!), Broccolesus crew, Krishnamurti, Woody Guthrie, Thelonious Monk, Barbara Hall, and the anamchara Paul Francis. To strawberries and all nouns starting with the letter *S*, everywhere.

CONTENTS

Foreword 1

Introduction 5

Kill Me So Much 13

Disguise 14

Ol' Green Eyes 15

The Coliseum 16

Banana 18

Dig 19

1 & 2 20

Numbers 22

Sink Her 25

Paper Tiger 27

What's the Word 31

Nocturne for Chopin 33

Sneaker 35

The State 37

A Valid Question Ensues Unstitched 38

Free Stallion 40

Plume 42

Pax Vobiscum 44

Anna 49

Beyond the Pale 50

Dear S. 55

Vibration 58

Moths 60

When 63

Pipe Dreams 65

Neil Tour 2003—Greendale Ends   68

Dear Divinity   69

Train   70

Truth About Dark   72

Celebrate   74

The Loneliest   78

About the Author   81

FOREWORD

I am happy to introduce the poetry of Amber Tamblyn to a wide audience. I hope readers will recognize that this is the work of no mere twenty-one-year-old, but of an exceptional young woman whose development as a poet must be both nurtured and anticipated.

In these works, one finds a voice grounded in life, everywhere struggling for liberty against the colonization of the mind and body, to a degree that is, at least, unusual and, at most, remarkable.

Remarkable in the sense that Tamblyn has already attained a distance from herself as an actress (and an accomplished one, at that), and is able to use her work in television and movies—with all the attendant "image" extensions—as content in a rebellious attack on all forms of commercialization that obstruct or violate the clear liberty that is for her the expression of her humanity in poetry.

So, these works are not from a hobby of crumbs left over from a loaf of fame and offered as a supplement to the big issue of Amber Tamblyn, superstar.

These poems are the real thing: the journey, the exploration, and the structuring of a woman in her growing pains and determination. Amber is among those who know that poetry is the most powerful human expression on Earth, and is dedicated to it like the sea is dedicated to the moon.

She has had around her from childhood an environment that has been open to, if not opened by, the arts. Her father, the noted actor and dancer Russ Tamblyn, is himself an excellent artist of collage. Her mother, Bonnie, is a woman of great range and depth as a singer of folk and popular songs, as well as a teacher in a local progressive school. The Tamblyn home has always been open to artists and poets of every stripe. Old friends like the artist-poet George Herms and the actor-artist Dean Stockwell, as well as renowned poet Michael McClure and myself, have been part of Amber's life since her birth. In addition, all of us are fraternally devoted to the memory of Wallace Berman, a verbo-visual artist who was killed in an automobile accident some years before Amber was born, but whose name has always floated about the Tamblyn home and into her ears because, if anything, Wally was a maker of poets. Amber has been writing since she was a child, and when she was sixteen, I had a poem of hers, "Kill Me So Much"—written when she was twelve—published in San Francisco's *Café* magazine. Even then she was showing signs of being a genuine creator. Later, she self-published a couple of chapbooks, circulating them among friends and schoolmates.

At the outset of 2004, she asked me to read with her at the Beyond Baroque cultural center in Venice, California. There, she astounded the crowd by reading her "Pax Vobiscum" poem, a tremendous homage to Woody Guthrie. Her feeling for Guthrie and for the proletarian story of America was exemplary, even astonishing for one so young. A couple of months afterward, that poem appeared in the "Beat Bush" issue of *Long Shot* magazine on the East Coast, edited by New York poet Eliot Katz. On the West Coast, her poem "Free Stallion" appeared in Csaba Polony's *Left Curve* magazine.

Those poems are part of this collection.

Other poems will reveal her liberating poetic spirit as well. Tamblyn writes from a core of forthrightness that is maturing with every poem. She's not afraid to take risks with the language, and in some of the poems—I'm thinking especially of the two parts of "Numbers" (perhaps because the theme is so close to her heart, i.e., the violation of the soul as well as the body of woman)— she really swings out the hammer of poetry in an exclamatory rally cry for justice.

There have been poets of high quality in the past who have had relationships with image-making machines like movies: Antonin Artaud acted in many films and wrote while he was doing so. Pier Paolo Pasolini was a great film creator and never stopped writing poetry. And I have had the honor also of translating Katerina Gogou, a marvelous poet who had appeared in Greek cinema and who wrote some of the most contemporary and provocative poetry in the Greek language.

Indeed, all three noted above were great poets because they were great provocateurs.

Amber Tamblyn's work is just now coming to light on the poetic horizon. However seminal, it already manifests elements of provocation that, for me, are the marks of a resonant importance in full development. These first steps are giant ones in that process.

—Jack Hirschman

INTRODUCTION

Introducing one's self is a difficult task. Talking about yourself in the narrative does not give a clear view of who you are; that is why I asked my dear friend Jack to write a more biographic opening. But what I found from the experience of putting this book together was an overwhelming sense of self-understanding, a sort of third-person love for whoever has been growing inside of me for years. I am blessed to be surrounded with the kind of love that does not cater to the spectacle of a career based on an image, as the entertainment business makes me feel at times. It's the kind of love that pursues and pushes the constant fine-tuning of an artist who funnels the truth through one woman's eyes. And my eyes have seen the best and worst of both worlds. This is what I hope to share with you through this collection of poems, *Free Stallion*.

I began writing poetry at a very early age, maybe about eight or nine years old. I wrote essays and short stories with my father, who heartily encouraged my budding imagination. Growing up, my parents surrounded me with the many creative influences they were fortunate to have, from artists like George Herms, Wallace Berman, Dean Stockwell, Bruce Conner, Ed Ruscha, Dennis Hopper, David Lynch, Neil Young, and many more. I watched and learned and, like a sponge, I absorbed everything around me. My father taught me that "the meaning of life is the search for the meaning of life," an expression that I live by when trying to write down something I cannot explain. The search is always the most important thing. He and my mother opened me up to philosophers, writers, and poets such as J. Krishnamurti, Deepak Chopra, Diane Di Prima, Walt Whitman, Pablo Neruda, Wanda Coleman, and Nietzsche.

Within the world of poetry, there was one person who stood as a rebel warrior for the sonnet of my conscience. Jack Hirschman, a man I emulated stylewise as a little girl, was the father figure and master in encouraging and training my existential concepts and views on womanhood, Hollywood, the death of a high school love, politics, and just about everything that has come my way to date. Jack was initially a professor of English at UCLA and has spent the rest of his life translating the telling work of poets all over the world. He translates in nine languages. Jack is a proletarian and an activist for the working class, and has a raw intuition on matters of the heart. He's a bear of a man, gentle, vibrant, and full of youthful energy, and he has a passionate love of life. Those who are fortunate enough to come into contact with him or hear him read poetry can be changed for life. Though he translates others, his best translation to date is one of human emotion into words of any kind—that is a spectacular gift.

My style has gone through many stages, and I am sure it will continue to do so. A few of the pieces are dream sequences. For example, the poem "Train" was inspired by a repeating dream about an experience

with a man I hated to love. I had been in a relation-
ship with someone who had not been fair to me. I
hated loving him because, in love, you have no con-
trol. Inside the dream his physical form changed from
a man to a horse, and I stood by and watched him get
hit by a train, while at the same time I *told* him to
cross the tracks. This dream was a very violent and
vivid experience, and would cause me to wake up in
a sweat. I still believe to this day that this was both a
fantasy and a nightmare, which is why, when the
dream repeated, the pleasure of beckoning him never
went away.

Because this book is a teenage timeline of sorts,
you will find some work I wrote when I was as young
as twelve years old. The poem I decided to put first in
this book, "Kill Me So Much," was written at that very
tender age. It was an homage to Jack and his politi-
cal voice. I wanted a voice like his, and I still get a kick
out of reading that poem. I believe I wrote it after
witnessing racism for the first time during the Rodney
King riots that took place in Los Angeles in 1992.
Also, the poem "Banana" is an example of my writing
style's first blossoming. This poem was written when
I was fourteen years old, and it has a lot of personal
significance as far as where I was physically and emo-
tionally during the time when I wrote it. It is a good
piece that shows the beginning of what I feel would
be my growth spurt as a writer.

"Pax Vobiscum," which means "peace be with
you," is a poem I wrote for Woody Guthrie, a man

who stood for the use of music and politics to fight governmental injustice and fascism in early-twentieth-century America; a man who used music for its true worth. I was possessed to write this poem after years of listening to stale, washed-out, pop culture music that I was subjected to throughout my teens. Tired of my generation's affected lack of constructive intent, I wanted to reach back to a time when there were people who found things in life that were worth fighting for. Except for a few artists who are relatively unknown, I have yet to find anyone in the mainstream whose music reflects his or her daily way of living. I have yet to see a music television artist that does not cannibalize a real activist's image in order to generate character interest before their album is released. It seems like everything is a marketing scam these days. As Johnny Rotten once said, "The best you can be in a positively backwards world is absolutely negative." Well, for some, "punk is dead," but the expression lives on and so does the hope for a modern-day Guthrie.

The haikus at the end are a shortened version of a book I did last year with artist George Herms, entitled *The Loneliest*, a series of poems and artwork dedicated to jazz legend Thelonious Monk. I was on the boardwalk at Venice Beach a while back and I saw a street artist painting a beautiful picture of a black man at a piano. When I asked how much he was selling it for, he snickered and asked if I even knew who the painted figure was. He would not sell this painting to a white girl from Santa Monica. I became obsessed with Monk, listening to *Straight, No Chaser*, watching the documentary of the same name, and learning everything I could about this musician out of sheer cultural embarrassment. I then had an internal Monk-related vision that lasted for more than two months, and I wrote a short poem or haiku about Thelonious almost every day. Later I spoke with George Herms about my obsession, only to find that he, too, was an avid Monk fan. Right then and there we spoke of the beginnings of what would end up being a poetry book/art collaboration. I still need to go see that man on the beach and trade him this product of my inspiration for that painting. He owes me. I suppose we owe each other.

These poems are moments. They make up a grander story than what I can explain here, in a good ol' intro section. So onward. Get cozy, and then let's get nosy. Enjoy.   —Amber Tamblyn

Free Stallion

KILL ME SO MUCH

The war has started,
the blood flags are raised high for us to see.
Die! Die! we all cry
with our stubborn cannons blowing off,
and our noses like dead poodles,
arriving on a nightmare,
praying for a dream.

Laughing at all those guts and bones on dream paper,
money that the Government is grieving over.

WE STILL WANT MORE RESPECT!
For the black, the rabbi, and the painters and the
    preachers.

WE STILL WANT MORE RESPECT!

All those computers
and typewriters
and digital phones,
all paid by rich men with their cannons blowing off,
and rich women with their noses like dead poodles.

WE STILL WANT MORE RESPECT!

And not just some buzzing bulb and a fly to keep it
    company.

DISGUISE

I'm in bed with the lights on,
the guise in plaid knee-highs
undercover in your underwear.
I'm writing the whole half of a lie
in story reform.
It's a freedom country if you dare
to know a girl in her heartland.

It's the agony of you chewing gum,
the way you say nothing but move your tongue . . .

OL' GREEN EYES

Be still my heart
in Autumn
you were a captured wild
Indian paintbrush has nothing on paintings like you,
or Indians.

All that heaved my chest lay there in your stems.
You had that push-up bra like a shield.
Who were you under there
engulfing my eyes?

It's brown against green,
this whole seasonal sexual thing's weighing down
my nipples' generosity.
They see you.
They both do

in Autumn,
you taught me to climb trees
to let the Fall
just fall.

THE COLISEUM

No framed photo holding amber love,
no rack to mount the swan.
Swan dies in the big picture,
big picture sees very little,
small AND few.
(Forget the song, Amber)
No meaning means no-thing,
everything has meaning but this, Amber,
(answer the bastard, Amber).
Enter the house made of bedposts
of frames you've slept upon
where hearts have bled through
staining a wood-stained floor
bleached out,
blacked out.
Eat the meat, make it right, Amber,
make the apology neutral
in between the lines,
in between your legs,
the lines on your legs stretch
marks already, at such a young age?

Insane already, the beer empty,
the life half there, Amber,

fill the rest.
Fill the rest,
crack the nut in you, Amber, crack her hard,
glue in the extra eyelashes,
admit to label prostitution,
GO ON!
Eat the meat, make it right.
In the coliseum slant
bodies, dressed for rich fog,
emeralds and rubies
(wear the meat, Amber),
as the seats puke forward, tumble down,
gowns and genitals, oh my gracious,
the glorious rust-belt of fame decapitated,
rusty pig urine running fearful from their torn holes
(smell the pigs, Amber),
death on the stage
as the coliseum eats itself from the outside in:
stage wins.

BANANA

Actress?
Yes, I am.
How did it happen?
Personally. Anyway
I'm always
a different person,
an accident
to them.

Could you say
you know me?

No, it's not my face
that pitches swift
serene kisses'
obliqueness
to mustaches of your likeness.
Script-typing
on the edge of fast,
my life
a stripe of reality
to be typecast.

DIG

Who pissed in the stream?
What's left to flow through conscience but caution.
A weary eye strains focus for substance snacks
and I'm giving meal penalties against the limelight.

Industry trashcans line my city limits
and plague my valleys with stench.
Seduction's a progression without the progressives.
Hollywood's got a face.
Trophy wives with stitched-up sideburns
look like 3rd degree burn victims.
There's a name and a body for every lie
walking without reason through my life: fire shadows.
I do not call this home.

She wants to eat but my plates are empty.
She says we'll all share the same grave.
I say why don't you
let me dig my own, ma?

1 & 2

1

Cross-country hearts on a CD-R,
there where a pen skipped a beat.
He forgot to color in a meaning.
For a man of one liners
he sure does a good line dance.

If, in fact, these are the seven shades of sage
on the color wheel of grays
then what a wheel of fortune to submit to!
It's a belligerent process to know him,
a card-shark swimmer playing streaks of blue-hair
     water.
Shades fade but
he'll never pale
and she'll never compare.

2

She wears lobster pajamas and writes with butane pens
as she spits out sparks helplessly.
Depression mentions cold feet
getting strokes of heat waves.

Her weathered eyes are cluster-fucks of confusing
　　road maps.
She's got a rabid hunger to be eaten
and there are many forks in the road,
nerves like dead ends,
curves that don't bend,
size 29 jeans for an ass that is barked for
on legs like redwoods,
her lumber is limber,
cameras flash and scream her name like "Timber!"
She collides with their kaleidoscopes,
they're just barking up the wrong tree stump.

It's a sketchy universe for shooting stars

refueling
rewriting
remiss.

NUMBERS

(Butcher 1)

Let go of that number,
that plasma will never have your eyes.
There'll be no golden hair or golden years.
That perfect consumptive repulsion
the decision demon taunts.
Hold on to your wet hair coarse with screams and puke
as you sit seared against the cold bed.
In the hospital courtroom, you push it out in front of
the grand jury surgeons all secretly hating you, maybe.

It takes away your seed, it does not take away the soil.

That number, that age, it cannot be saved,
hold on to a fraction of this image, if you dare,
if you can.

(Butcher 2)

Demon goes in deep with cullet for your gullet
as your puss-eye stands stern and frightened.

They take away your rights,
they do not take away your seed.

A voice will not be heard.
The number, the law of
butcher externally demanding entrance
to internally slaughter wombs of womankind.
Forcefully silencing my bladder's laughter,
soldering its hangnail to my lining,
slamming her against the bed frame in tasteless violence
(fucking but no cutting in this particular "rule").

SLAY my entrance way, make it beg for saturation!
MURDER mother's dying roped neck contagious with
    questionable fingerprints!

MASSACRE temples built on private land
not standing erect enough for your "city standards"!
Let go of all numbers!

SLAUGHTER my eyes, makeshift them weeds to crush
    beneath God's brow, as I might beg for benediction!

EXECUTE cute and cuddly,
forced ejection results in physically miasmic uglies!

DESTROY the woeful wolf, keep the number fractal!

EXTERMINATE my crowning with a clawed quill pen's
        punctuating and puncturing!

DESTROY Roe the wage-ist, collect her dues and
sew that slit up until the 9th!

KILL the voices haunting 16 coats 15 coat hangers!

BUTCHER the buss of blessing femininity
in sequence!
In fact, slaughter that number!
Be that hunter!

The murder that was NOT a federal case of morality,
        a woman's spirit!
You think to yourself: maybe
God is a realist with no Christian friends.

SINK HER

I love the smell of your morning breath hovering over
my face in a dolled-up dawn chill,
against a light-blue haze that drags the daylight kicking
and screaming in.
My velvet-covered raspberry heart
grows hooks to snag the meaning of intertwining
when words mean nothing but breathing.

I whisper to your butterflies down there:
Did you say something?
Would you say the words
that might prevent
the soft spot in my mouth from getting old?

I watch your fingernails grow, dirt and all,
never question where the time has gone because,
I pray secretly, it goes into small footsteps the likes of us.

It's a first strike for my love letters.
It's a home run for your unopened mail.

This is the pond I built,
this the stream I wallow in
memories so hot they burn down fires.
I want to force you
to force me
to do something against my will,
measure you like a measurement of hell;
from my ankles you grapple

to the space between my hipbones
Dizzy like Rascal from your spin zones.
I'm the hard evidence that
your indifference shreds.

Battery acid turns to crème.
Love unveils an 80-year dream
which is really
just a plan without an instinct.
You got me doing the doggy paddle, upstream,
hook,
line,
sink her.

PAPER TIGER

I should stop dreaming.
If God has a head,
Earth's the bad tooth to get pulled.
He should pull it,
count his losses,
and smile.

Easy is the defamation of the grandest mother.
Her tranquility goes under with blood-drenched rocks
like blisters, pox o' man's apocalypse.
She sweats to detoxify us,
she's pushing with wood-worn arms,
slivering the tips,
reaching, throwing those
silver hooks out of her water basins.
She's blowing with mighty lip, nuclear acid-baths
trapped in cloud bubbles, out of a charged atmosphere
     that just might pop
when the next cigarette is lit,
when the next can is bent.

She should stop denying
fish running pregnant with Hg.
The bad water breaks
delivering bloody womb-tumors like babies.
The President's got promises of dead zones:
Overflowing with raw sewage!
Saturated with pesticides and human bone!
He's shooting up lobbyist green and

shitting out greenhouse gasses!
Omitting the CWA and CAA for the RNC and the NRA,
muzzling and punishing scientists like pound-bound strays,
grinning through brown, striped plaque all the way to
    the bank.
He's dining on my generation's decaying flesh,
making sweet meals out of our last natural resources,
saying "cheers" to corporate capitalism,
rubbing his swollen stomach of stench
while the crust of my ancestors becomes stale in the
    crevices of his rot hole,
using my future as a toothpick!

No mercy for mercury!
No history for human legacy!

She is torn from river to liver,
ripping road lights and track housing stapled to her tits,
grids of land waste,
cities stacked upon dead cities like moldy metal,
a robot's cum shot.
Animals are being born to breathe factory poison
feeding off their own guts and lungs.
We eat that slaughter!
We digest the masticated reincarnated
and call it a "happy meal".
Smithfield Foods will feed you the unknown because,
quite frankly,
the cows will never come home.

About those bubbles:
The horizontal wheeze of the planet extends.
The "Golden Triangle" still burns like
the third eye of an acrid fortune.
Yes, the preview is fluorescent at twilight,
the devil's spit permeates coal-soaked earth.
The EPA is MIA,
defenseless as laws are lifted.
The sky grows dark and the heat grows nails
tearing away the envelope
that the world was so mysteriously handed to us in.

This administration lets
a piece of Houston die to this inferno.
Chevron names an oil tanker after board member
Condoleezza Rice.
The irony cannot be dismissed.

National Mercury Providers
call to action those callouses of lies we've grown.
Suppression of Dissent!
Refuse to negotiate with corporate environmentalism!
Raise fists of new clear proliferation against cronyism,
blow by blow, voice by voice!
Let Mother deliver rapid spankings to those white asses:
The Gale Nortons
Dick Cheneys
Samuel Bodmans
and Karl Roves!

Let the disciples walk a million miles
in death's shoes!
Let the hogs scuff over the last piece of bacon!
Let the paper tigers weep over their pussy bills,
screaming tarnation over their tar-filled nation's landfills!

The other side IS greener, my friends,
the lawn is calling for some kind of picket,
and it ain't a fence, my friends, no,
there'll be no stopping of dreams!
There'll be no happy pill-fillers reading:
"Avoidance, brought to you by the makers of denial!"

Mother has seen the daughter sit,
and watched the sun set,
her family eroded,
the human race in an awkward state
apologizing for missing teeth.

WHAT'S THE WORD

Destiny calls,
despair ruffles
these wrists the
only hands I know,
drowning their mistakes
in some damn cold
(damn fine)
water.

Webster's dictionary
3 a.m.,
phototropic me
in limbo,
his existence still wins
satiating a begrudged fantasy.
It's no mare's nest
enveloped in a green,
monotonously pulsing symphony:
       it's your green eyes
       I do recall.
Night's marked
cruel self-depictions,
the western hemisphere imbedded with emeralds,
an angry appetite
to stop your luster,
my green house crashing
at your beckoning.

Come, call me, baby,
    I wanna break it all.
        Love is crumbly anyway.
            I'll crumble with you.

Call me, baby,
any-which-way,
any damn fine way
you please.

At peace,
that's me,
with hating myself
over you.

A word. Your number
redialing. On hold.

            Limbo,
                damn fine limbo.

NOCTURNE FOR CHOPIN

Spectacular?
Yes, it's
the gift,
memory soft and sorrowful,
that keeps on giving
those keys you play.

I see you've studied me,
distant chamber,
reaction of tears
on these weary cheeks,
years cried
weeping music sheets,
nights hazy with your finger train,
a sleepy howl
to the moon's erogenous behavior.
Your theories are clever,
you played my teens
in perfect pitch
scaling my longings,
I slept to your time callings
hinting at all those memories
before I lived them,
blue adolescence,
young fear growing
painfully exciting and wondrous,
night would call,
I'd come,
you played softly in the dark.

Good God, kissing your mystery
is a delicacy.

Night would call
and I'd run.

SNEAKER

Saturn's in his eyes tonight.
206 is not definable as he opens the hotel door for this
    perfect stranger
and takes a backseat to her giggle.
They play chess on the bed, but there are no pawns.
There's strategy in the ceiling painting but no paint,
the language is filled with spoonerisms
reflecting 2 spoons yawning,
his fingers guaranteeing switch-blade voodoo
as he cuts cookies from her heart
to save in his cookie jar.

The bandit stole tickets to her sneak preview.
She's a foreign film without subtitles
in a drowned-out basement
with no seats and kisses in wide-screen.
He basks in her turquoise and turns the air bashful when
the bridge of his finger brushes her ear.
His minor scale weighs a generous voice, a giving man.
She doesn't sugar-coat suggestion
and suggests he sing more often.
(what a life is made in 4 hours when talking's tangible!)
If she fell asleep,
his rib cage would devour and swallow
injections of her punctuation;
her cup-holder hips keep his juices flowing and
reject fantasy with true love and honesty.

He will leave chessboard and all
through the tunnels of their percussion.
Strangers go marching one by one.
What begets premonition has not begun,
like leaving the table light on; a one night-stand.
She watches his story become history
and she's just a fable.

Conception smiles.
The affect bares teeth and laughs.
Affection doesn't sneak,
it strides.

THE STATE

The state of the weight of music:
the lid don't fit over boys
threatenin' to balance out faces crooked
now, does it?

That promise-ring stalls
an actual engagement of the mind,
promised soldiers fire guns from mouths.
Those guns are tired now,
bought ammunition,
enslaved and engaged
to the competitive market
of social shock-and-awe buffers.
The numbered decree given proof
sets sail the last American ships,
a convoy of depleted rhyme-sayers,
poets despondent.

Letter pens tucked, techs drawn,
gunpowder showers from their nostrils,
the tick tick of sirens coming to life,
all this fighting for the proper burial of a servant,
a despondent poet.

Last rapper's got a bad rap
as hip-hop's suicide is forgotten.

A VALID QUESTION ENSUES UNSTITCHED

No, your clothes are cute
but a faze to me,
a poisonous recipe.
I watch out
for those kinda snacks.
My stitches are early scratches,
semi-seam lines,
uncontrollable scars.

You make honey cakes
a mummy's thought on fatalism
practicing preservation skills
on a jelly-filled lady roll
for a woman
with no jiggle at the end of her tailbone.

How am I to fit into your bulimia?

Unzip my curves'
voluptuous secret,
petty bone right below my womb.
You silence it
with fabric of fabrications,
treaties deceitful to my gallant ancestry.
What images do you hold?

Not mine!

How am I to fit into your bulimia?

Don't know what else to tell you—
I love pizza.

FREE STALLION

Wet pavement makes me yawn,
    a cat out of slumber,
dreams rumble
whiskers
memories whisper
cold kisses my spine-time-line
broken railroad track
crossing refuge of a century turned bitter,
empty trains
belt out silent crossings,
ghosts tap-dance out a beat like:
nothing is wrong
nothing has died
no short is long
no tears have cried

swinging
head to heart
heart to hand
hand to head,
it's a disaster,
bloodstream's a circus freak
turning tricks,
female inherence replicating

an equestrian prayer,
a woman running, free stallion

as I like to call it, yes,

free stallion

a bottle of jack and the night is a coward
coming
going
kissing and telling
climbing into my sheets
never calling before arriving
raiding my fridge
never calling the day after
leaving socks on the dresser
sexing me when it's good for me
hitting me when it's best for me
apathy when the end is bleak
when night skips sheets
not my lover but just another
momentary treat
a love seat
minus 1

what innocent free stallion?
what innocence

PLUME

Raw war
too bloody for taste
tastes like born-again/death wish.

Raw war
genes of generations
momma's vertebra no longer vertical,
scattered like shrapnel
far and wide.

Raw war
the fat needle
the bomb-ass drug,
dazed and uneducated
Sam sweeps secrets under his peruke.

Vomit
he infects me
the thinking thing
nature's unwanted trademark
selfish, sandy,
rubbing rustily,
fuck me verbally,
slowly,
exclamation point,

the dot of misery.

The whitest plume
raw war
the fat needle,
insert here,
globalization is erect,
love floundering, outdated and discontinued.

PAX VOBISCUM

(last love song for Woody Guthrie)

You've been here before
here now ever last
poetic proletarian
lost
bloodshot
eyes
frostbitten against
ties that dye, red maybe
decades of you,
pauper, seed-planter,
the infamous struggle you watched,
fighting was no option
but absolute.

I dreamt I kissed you,
it was 1934,
dust was popular,
populists a scarce disease,
the first red flag
warning discovered
you, my hero,
battling sensationalism,
the queer concept/institutionalism

the form
of America
'n' all them
poli-TISH-ns.

I dreamt I was the last
catching a glimpse,
your freedom fields
wind blowing agitation running wild
in your eyes frostbitten.

I could make love to your memory,

the prosaic figures of my youth
less the equivalent
of strings you have strummed,
those battles you won
this dream, merciless transcendence.
I wake caution, she sleeps too much,
national continuous slumber
I'm dwelling/dying in it.

Where have you reincarnated?
Did you birth anew?
Where are the lost songwriters
of you?

Woke up,
dreamt I was the last,
wept for my country,
she's so confused.
It was 2003.

We've been here before
you and I
singing
fascism the joke,
the ha-ha of ironic unfolding.
/
History is reality is future,
Lomax was there,
he taught me F sharps,
fire-illuminated
Thomas Hart Benton paintings airbrushed into your
    wrinkles
the most astonishing portrait,

patriotism as individual,
a sight not even Maxim Gorky could describe,

Communism's true definition
I could contemplate
your meanings.

Early America
you tried to salvage,
you beauty, you,
the passion molding an infinity's heart
before us
among us
against us
beyond us.

No one sees you,

a voice provocative,
a recording/distilled ideology
crepitating gestures, pictures curling,
ages moving,
morals washing
away.

I still see you,
night time sings me
my own dust-bowl ballads
like searching scars in the dark:

In love we trust,
in time we rust,
the man
the legend
predestined prophet
words like pollen rest heavy in this amber,
it's a metaphor
like 1934.

Dove, where have you reincarnated?
Are you laughing in disgust somewhere?
Did you birth anew?
Where are the lost leaders
of you?

Guthrie

I'm gushing

America

the "once was" story

manifestation of all destinies

turquoise nation forgave us too soon

time

half of me

pax vobiscum.

ANNA

In the dusk partial and complete, you drop in
behind the dripping melon-colored marquee.
The fault title font fronts a fruit-cup decay
with your name all over it.

Drunk in that love cup,
blood-berry strong in that heart's garden,
saffron kisses in heavenly 1930s night skies, as dusk
    may give you away
to eternity,
to the sky,
to the garden.

Drunk in that love cup,
you imagined the sunset and fled to it,
chin up, eyes straight.

I craved that fruit today,
my birthday,
2 days before you passed away
up into the sky.

BEYOND THE PALE

No poem
or word
was good enough
for her.

She melted ingredients
cared little about
our little-hood,
she was breeding in a barren bakery
Poes and Millays,
her brow erupted
spectacular shock
breaking the horizon behind.

Her face
orange rusty pear
hair strangely tamed
frozen fire in mid-explosion
eyes tunnelled in
gaping endearment
reaching out
magnetized to our immunity
the spider captured our imaginations
in the web of her allowances

for the most part

crying at the notion
owning individuality
a crucifying possession.

She never took never
for an answer, did she?

I questioned her rigid speaking,
hated her for academic archaism, with a spring in
     her step

she read
A Wrinkle in Time
our minds captivated
in elusive difference
daydreaming
this crack-house public school
had a prizewinning ghost
erected from the basements
to scare us
into loving her
and face a public disability
known to us as constructive criticism.

She found me annoying
overly ambitious
a stumbling linguist,
cerebral writing
came un-ruled and wild

swerving from my pen
misspelled
misused,
she fell for
my slapdash liberty
reckless loyalty to love poem-fodder.

No one
listened
the way she did

above all the others,
my spoiled life to her,
beyond the pale.

Her wisdom predicated
a hungry soul
bound to keep me
from an easy choice,
a fool's choice

"acting career."

Yes, the Paraclete
raised me with loving arms
sobbing fingers
afraid the written me
was a future nonentity.

She never forgave me

for punishing her persistence,

an unspoken failure
most notable
at the last moment
of her last year there,
no bittersweet utter
"I'm so proud of you"
"I'll miss you"
as she slipped through
cracked unpainted hallways,
through 3 generations of apprentices
left half empty
to color in a life's work
half done,

the ironic beauty
demure banana posture walking
out the doors
my school my heart
battered haunted by her mystification,
the most painful daze.

I never did what she dreamt.
She's a butterfly now
or maybe a moth, yes,
hopelessly stuck to my subconscious light
batting wings grey and brown,
flagging me down.
Remember the hard times, she would say.
What I taught you, she would whisper.

Sometimes I see her
walking past my house
smiling talking of sunsets and such things,
deeply involved, unaware
as I drive by
unseen.

The crusted-over scar
peels a little.
She makes the pink poke through.
Freeze frame.

Her punishment lives on
driving on,
taking me nowhere.

DEAR S.

There you lay in the hospital coiled up in pink sheets.
I dreaded coming here for weeks now
to face you and your new friend, Death.
You both stare waiting for me to commit to my grief
    and let you go,
but I can't let you go.
I hate that you smiled, ever.
You let me into your heart, and house with crumbling
    walls and caving ceilings,
you let me make fun of your laugh and be mean with
    admiring intentions,
you let me cry in selfishness when you broke the news,
and offered no tears to partner with,
you let me share the stars in the sky and your eyes
and the days crashed and the waves passed,
you let me love you for a second before you
handed me the knife and requested a turning favor,
you let me be your mother,
hate you for being so young,
miss you before you were gone.

Now I see that door.
I'm blood in a hallway like a vein
strung from your death grip.
All veins lead to your heart
and I'm pumping hard.

I could tumble over my remorse for not coming sooner
and fall right into your hands.

You're quiet now,
white and gold.
Yes, I remember this body
but not the face.
That halo still sits above your bed and that head like an
     elevator shaft.
Angels sit selfishly awaiting your skyscraper-arrival.
I will not return you to whoever gave you to me,
I can't.
So you will leave truly alone,
your bier built into my chest like ancient stone.
The floors are clean,
the curtains drawn.
I'll say goodbye without saying it.

Who's gonna take that toe ring you danced all night on?
Who's gonna keep your writings and sob over their
     forecast?
Who's gonna smell your absence in your clothes and
     burn them,
those jeans we played mischief in?
Give them to the army surplus store (I couldn't do your
     figure justice).
Who's gonna blow wishes with my fallen eye-lashes?
Who's gonna come that close to my face, ever?
Who'll take my breath away just by breathing?
Who'll silence me just by being?

Dear S., dance with me in the dark of your familiar.
Let's touch swan-like for a last time, in this hour,
wrap necks and
coo (your favorite word).
I'll say it
without saying it.

VIBRATION

Our love spilt,
hate left the stain.

Touch march.
I'm holding an anarchist's stance at the rally of your
        neglect.
I'm standing on the front line of the protest,
I'm picketing with signs high in front of your think tank.
You're gonna have to run me down,
to really run away.
My blood slogans will not go unanswered this time.
The message pulls focus:
yes, the meaning is clear—
I'm chaining myself to our memories,
you don't need a key to release me.
Riot gear shields you from my kisses like
tear gas makes your cheekbones run interference and
my voice screams for a crowd of thousands in a
        singular note.
Scar tissue should be outlawed.
Battle marks are for the brokenhearted.

This
is the woman's right to choose.

You split up my soul-vibration like packaged meat,
for every public eye to have a piece and eat.
You served me up
cold and raw.

My headlines have become the wallpaper inside
    your burning house
where I watch you penetrate a desert of my ashes,
one mole at a time.

Correct this death penalty,
I demand it.
Drop your weapons—
pick up my hip attachment.
Screw it,
on.
I'm suing for a-sexual harassment.

MOTHS

I consider myself flexible in awkward positions.
Not a home wrecker,
but I do knock.
And you and I are pals.
The kind that
open up to each other but keep mouths
at a safe distance.

But I cannot amend all tongues.

I walk the dubious centerfold of your eye-line, friend.
I carry my purse on the same side you walk next to me
to avoid hand.
To avoid saying anything small.
We are the shredded fuse,
the rebound wires commencing,
badly rerouted and iniquitous.
We are the failed test of the emergency buddy system.
Chums.
I am a derelict without furniture or life signs,
painting your posture from distance that
can fit inside the palm of your land.

Though we share ice cream instead of pipe dreams,
I know

you'd never be lover to another poet
because you are one.
And the fear of being served a reflection
in the way that you have served some,
is a glass house you are not ready to escape from.
I'll keep liking mint, while you go for chocolate.
Conundrums
I can't seem to get away from.

You are just another sheep
jumping the fence in my nightmares.
Counting out numerical complacency,
a platonic answer with a nod-off.
Like a million hairs you've grown near your mouth
plowed down, rough and sore
my beard too wants to be a little roughed and worn, but

the time is not now, if not ever.
Not before, during, or after
her, your lover, another, or the next chapter.
So let's just say,
let's just stay
friends, forever.

There is no title for our book cover-up,
so I will keep reading like a brood kept laboring.

Take a long walk off my short feet,
my stomach pleads hunger no matter
how much I eat

and its open mouth aches.
Where there should be butterflies there are moths
eating through my loins like loincloth.
If there's a map to things spoken, friend,
we'll see we are way off.

Buddies.
You're the worst kind because
you won't even reject me physically,
we can't even celebrate celibacy.
I am your dirty washboard
and yet have never had you inside me.

There's no declaration in our country.

Pals.
You tug the one red string
that seems to run through everything.

I seek your flying patterns from behind,
the blue leading the blind.

Friends. No beneficiary.
So we stay.

WHEN

When my mother dies
I'll smoke my first cigarette of at least a thousand
that will inevitably end my life.

I will not make the bed, but turn down the sheets;
white wind hands will
paint her face away, I will not
wear white.

Ashes will descend upon time
and time turn to dust.
Dust will appear forgivable and blue.

I never will notice until "warning" turns her light on
(Leave the light on, please),
I will do this nightmare a dirty favor
for my own peace and demise.

I will not recall Christmas décor.
Pink plastic lights
strung by papa's hands will not show
the twinkle in my short circuit.
I will not remember how
the blue ones gave away her grace,
with a foreshadowing too early for my liking,
as she stood in the kitchen
and made me eyes from scratch
to see through.

I will walk in circles around that wine stain

on the carpet floor.

I will not look for 7 a.m. sunlight squares
through the kitty door,
over-easy eggs and bacon
(kitty is long gone now).

I won't remember holding sermon on her chest,
sternums lain to rest,
mommy lying there without me
as I will be without my self.

I will string beads like spiderwebs
from this melting neck,
turquoises and pearls of hers,
and I will let them stay
a part of my body, as I
could not be.

I will not hear those songs I promised I would learn
but let die, those pipes in memory,
selfishly.
Guitars will invoke that nothingness
where a girl once sang along to a woman's chorus
in natural cause
that harmony remain sacred.

I will not remember, my ear to her stomach,
sounds of that blood moving.

When moo is gone,
I'll just let hair be hair. And hang there.

PIPE DREAMS

Truth is a tactic
a means to distortion,
see, on the shores of my beach
your abetting technique is a tidal wave
drowning out figures,
girls in disfigurement,
the liquidated body
a shape fit for a penis,
this the business of commercial muscle,
a community anxiety,
a syndrome of panic,
a "network" enforced disease
complete with glam and glit,
a death wish—hold the cheese!

Pipe dreams for women
the last remaining it seems
the last eating
breathing
the last full circle shred,
dump-truck worthy.

Ladies, they want to see bones,
softness is intimidating,
curves exceed the "standard" of unique,
too much of us
comes off too healthy,
vulnerability is "in,"
suffering is sensuous

a child of exquisite molestation,
smallness opens awkward indications of neediness,
small holes needing protrusion,
exposing a dark metaphor,
Moss taught us.

You want more bones?
Check a graveyard, I'm still living.
Have just recently taken a woman's form,
damn proud,
yes, this ass is mine.
I didn't eat my way here.
This is how we look, you must've forgotten.
Note to all you fashion queens:
backstabbing comments are a modern corset
set to break ribs, the last remaining,
the last cage guarding
ages of hips available for viewing
at your local theatre or high school.

Pipe dreams for women
the last remaining
last eating
believing,
dump-truck worthy.

So remember this:
a woman's body is not trademarked,
the standard is a corporate decision,
girls buy the image,
die to be it.

I'll die
before I live it.

I'm my mother's daughter,
take it or leave it,
no sucking in for squirting out
jerks, I am your greatest tear-jerker,
hexing your desires.
I'm my mother's daughter,
I carry every weight
of every Blanchard,
gaunt makes me giggle
but never pause.

NEIL TOUR 2003—GREENDALE ENDS

A dismal sanctuary
no, really
sometimes I hate LA
like a teenage rebel
I want to sneak out
in the night,
do stupid things with nature
in the dark,
regret them
in the light,
remember the good times,
then dread coming home with
hickey imprints,
a life dreamt in dreading
chains.

I am skin,
let's begin.

DEAR DIVINITY

Sucking on you
    E Z
years of my mouth
dry
displeased

empty decades
bottomless shameful flower blossoming
life is coming
in full fear

Your legs, my dear,
effortless
    you make me wanna write back-words
        time
            same
                the
                    at
                        pencils
                          two
                            with

TRAIN

(Libra continued)

Nightmares,
yours, or are they mine?
I see them through your eyes.
What I did
repeats.

Hide out in me,
then we'll both disappear
because it's ours.

A younger you
approaching the railroad between us.
I smile coyly: Come here,
you're becoming a horse,
you're blood-cut stars dripping into
legs of a man
I cannot stand
to adore.

Riding your raw back,
imagination shifting in rapid eye-movement,
your stall-fed mouth poking hard into
dark space.

You're becoming it—
that beast I kissed.

This image
repeats:

younger blood bay, you,
skull elongated thick and tough,
a jaw bone in need of flesh
(perhaps you want mine),
a twisted man/animal rabid for my apology
being dragged under the steel of a freight train,
dragging your hooves open over the steel
     like paper shells
the   image   repeats.

Your tangled pinks and veins rise up,
black-blood pupils reach for my face (oh, so distrusted!),
a muzzle like shattered jelly,
your choke caw slithers,
your squawk plea pounds,
to find my eyes
closed.

You beg for an explanation half alive as
your body unfolds in lush decay
all over my guilt.

My words ripple:
Stand there,
wait for the train.

TRUTH ABOUT DARK

Dark has rationed out his last patience.
Power's out.
Apocalyptic coming starches a manic
blood-hungry rainstorm on my driveway
    like
a harpy's tongue inviting
all that is outside
in

Darkness   still.

Wind is searching
for a decided feeding,
hairy, unseen.

It's coming for me.

Shadows come for me—
the mediocre poet.
I wrote your heart to be dead
and they know it.

No, night is not beautiful.
It's not for lovers or romances,
not for sexual advances
or carriage rides in the park.

No, dark still
is not for screaming stars
imprisoned in obliqueness
begging for forgiveness.
Night is not the trusted ear
nor the comforting friend.

Inside flesh is not pink:
black and lonely without artificial light,
tunnels of barren soiled skin like seaweed.
A forest without streetlight
is not naturally physically healing.

Lost in the bulrushes,
it is the thicket of a murderer's hair
through which the wind weaves its fingers
    before slaughter,
tall and constant,
never moving,
torturous,
awaiting stains of my grief
on his mustache and comb,
a revenge of its own
at its core
for no eyesore
bores deeper
than darkness.

Layers of dead lizards will
spook the harpy!
Hell's hole is in my moccasin.

CELEBRATE

Today I celebrate your death,
like a comedy of err.
They say the Lord takes you when he wants to,
but the sound of your heart stopping was his laughing.
What would he want with your heart
that I did not pump?
What could he take from your body
that I did not touch?

I still question a motive of universal character.
Your disappearing act left heavy lips for
displacing my teens and swinging me sexually.

Was it sexual?
Do eyes like these grow on trees?
It's funny now, I can hide a secret:
I will never lift the curse it took to keep it.

Today I project exaggerations,
intimacy and vulnerability,
catty remarks of two sixteen-year-olds who couldn't
     spell
adjusting to snow on the west coast while
the pleasure of disaster still hailed the fall.

Somewhere between
tucking your hair behind your ears
and your fingertips rubbing behind mine—
they might have called it a kiss,
I might have called it a talk.

A damning conversation.

Today I celebrate your blood
which spilled into tubes that
fed life into my mouth like rocks,
draining cascades from your father's vanity,
who beat you senselessly but owned you domestically.

Purchasing a loss of innocence
without posting a reward.

There through the halls of your home
I crept in nightly on inexperienced heels
to meet an experiment in discretion.
That cry when I held you from his sledge rage,
    that sound
later I would mistake for a moan.
It was
shortness of breath from a split lip
to new sounds in diary pages
that you never meant to show me.
But you did.
And it revealed it lasted longer than the drug that
    wore off.

Today I celebrate you leaving me, physically.

Before it got too serious.

Before I could explore the mystery.
Before something drastic changed in me.
Before we made plans to change the world by
      having babies.
Before I could climb under your covers easily.
Before we could admit to an anniversary.
Before we grew old and wise
and realized
we had the same color hair
and birthmarked thighs.
Before we used the same name to apply for things.
Before we made wedding rings out of string beans.
Before our souls might've made bondages.
Before we said things with our hands
and our words made pinky promises.

Today I laugh in your honor.
These tears are
glass trophies for
every year you spent
learning how to spell my name.
Write to me,
"Things don't last forrever, Strawberry."
Forever, with two r's,
like the word denied itself,
like the Lord prepared himself

to sit and face you in
a damning conversation
and finalize, a wish come blue.

I am now
so old next to
your high-school shadow.
On the lockers, in the corners, all their smiles.
Happy
6th Anniversary.

THE LONELIEST

Thelonious Monk
You play, the ism is theism
The loneliest Monk

Beneath the coffin
here lies the fetus of Monk
the layer has shed

De Soto exit
The crow caws at the red light
in sync with your keys

Getty Museum
A cat glorifies his style
copy cat, that is

B sharp the slick note
Give credit where credit's due
That b is for Blue

Big Bear streams live play
rhythm beats holes through spaces
Such heart in your pawse

Try to remember
the last time you played that song

to will out a ghost

Budakhan Mindphone
Squarepusher and the Monk must
share the same rib cage

In a dream last night
Ferncliff spit you up to play
for Garland and X

On Venice boardwalk
he paints your face red unknown
the color intrigues

My question disgusts
trite uncultured white girl thing
Who's Monk? he repeats

Liza, your stanza
She's distracting, isn't she?
Gets me every time

Red haze freeway curves
a nuclear orange sky
industrial sherbet

Dawn crawls on crutches
your verbal wedding ring, lost
in the rosewood strings

ABOUT THE AUTHOR

Amber Tamblyn is the star of the critically acclaimed CBS television drama *Joan of Arcadia*. She is also known for playing Emily Bowen-Quartermaine on the soap opera *General Hospital*, on which she appeared from 1995 to 2001. Amber's film work includes starring in Warner Bros.' *The Sisterhood of the Traveling Pants* as well as the cult hit *The Ring*.

Amber has been politically active for many years, working with such organizations as moveon.org, the ACLU, and Declare Yourself, and serving as a board member on Rock the Vote.

Amber's father is actor/artist Russ Tamblyn. Her mother, Bonnie Tamblyn, is a teacher and a seminal influence in establishing a human development program called Counsel in schools across America. Amber lives in Los Angeles. Visit her at www.amtam.com.

CPSIA information can be obtained at www.ICGtesting.com
Printed in the USA
LVOW11s1707250215

428344LV00001B/10/P